The Hen with the Wooden Leg

English edition copyright © 1992 by The Child's World, Inc.
French edition © 1988 by Casterman
All rights reserved. No part of this book may be
reproduced or utilized in any form or by any means
without written permission from the Publisher.
Printed in the United States of America.

Distributed to schools and libraries
in Canada by
SAUNDERS BOOK CO.
Box 308
Collingwood, Ontario, Canada L9Y 3Z7
(800) 461-9120

ISBN 089565-751-1
Library of Congress Cataloging-in-Publication Data
available upon request

The Hen

with the

Wooden Leg

author/illustrator: Claudine Routiaux

The Child's World
Mankato, Minnesota

The sun has not yet come up. Outside, a blizzard is raging. Judy, Pauline and Lorie are getting breakfast ready. Suddenly Cuddles, the dog, barks to go out.

"That's odd," says Grandpa, in surprise, "I'll go and see what's up," he calls out, sinking into the snow as he follows in the dog's tracks.

Pushed along by a great gust of wind, he soon
comes back in, carrying a shapeless bundle.

Mud — snow — blood — brr — a beak — a
foot — one eye — no, two! "It's a hen!"
choruses the family.

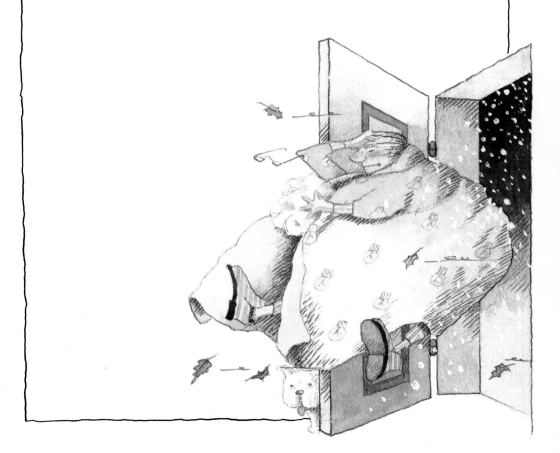

"She's lost one of her feet!" Pauline's sad discovery inspires Grandpa, however. He goes into his workshop, and… Bang!
…Thump!…Crack!…"Ouch!…Ouch!"

A few minutes later, and here he comes, carrying a sheer work of art in his hands. It's a carved wooden foot, and the admiring girls quickly set about fitting it to the poor hen's leg.

Almost at once they hear a loud stomach rumble.

"She must be hungry," decides Pauline.

But Grandpa is already at the stove, and…

Forgetting how weak she is, the hen stands up, and
hop! hop! she's got both feet in a plate of corn and
gobbles it up in a few beakfuls.

"Now, tell us about yourself," asks Pauline. "What's your name?"

"I'm called Orie," answers the bird.

"Orie!" exclaims Lorie, "What fun, you're just short an L, compared to me!"

"And you're just short a pair of wings, compared to me," retorts the bird, "Right?"

"Right," agrees Lorie, giggling. "So tell us what happened. How did you get hurt?"

"Well, it was like this:

Soon after I was hatched, my sisters and I were brutally chicknaped by a gang of infamous chicken thieves. We were taken in cages to a huge shed, where we soon met the boss, Crocker. He examined us, counted us, and sorted us into groups.

A few months later, when my sisters had started to lay eggs regularly, he went through the same process with their eggs. I was soon facing the facts: I was the only hen not producing any eggs: the outlook for my future was looking bleak.

Things came to a head yesterday. Since morning Crocker had been prowling about among the cages, with a nasty look in his eyes and a hatchet in his hand. Outside, a blizzard raged. The wind was howling, there was a fight going on between the sky and the earth. I had a feeling that there was a fight going on in the keeper's head too. I was right. I saw him coming toward me, waving his hatchet. He angrily yanked the door of my cage open, but just then a branch hit the skylight so hard that the glass broke. The light went out. Crocker cursed and stumbled over backwards.

I quickly hopped from my cage, jumped up to the skylight, and crashed through it. By the time I hit the ground I was in such terrible pain that I fainted: my foot had been severed by a piece of broken glass. I managed somehow to get across the fields and woods. By dawn I was exhausted, and I collapsed. The snow soon covered me. It would have been the end of me if that fine animal had not found me."

Everybody turns to look admiringly at Cuddles, and he gets a double helping of bones and hugs.

"That little creature's not too bad after all," Cuddles mumbles.

"How can we catch those hen thieves?" wonders Judy, concerned.

"I have a scheme," says Orie, "Get me an old sheet, a camera, a suitcase, and…off we go to the shed. I'll show you the way, with Cuddles' help."

Finding the way back is not so easy in the snow. Forward, backward, to the left — no, to the right. The little band is having trouble getting along. Suddenly, rounding a bush, Orie quivers:

"Over there, look! Behind the trees — that horrible building — that's the shed!"

There Orie goes, rushing forward, scrambling up the tree, and then clinging bravely to the skylight. In a few cluck-clucks, she explains her scheme to the hens below, as she displays the bed-sheet, now turned into a banner showing these words for all to read:

GREAT EGG STRIKE

"You wait," she whispers, as she climbs down again, "Just come back again tomorrow!"

The next day, enraged, Crocker is yelling:

"This is the limit! Not a single egg! We're ruined. All this fine feathered lot will end up in the pot, and you can get ready for the biggest chicken heist you've ever seen. I want all the trucks ready by midnight!"

Meanwhile, Judy is hiding all the hatchets in the suitcase, Pauline is discreetly taking pictures, and Lorie is murmuring to Grandpa:

"With all this evidence all we need is for Detective Jones to meet the trucks at midnight — and these bandits will be nabbed."

And indeed, the next morning, Detective Jones holds a news conference and announces:

"All the chicken thieves are under lock and key, ladies and gentlemen, thanks to this little hen with the wooden leg."

Orie and Pauline throw their wings and arms around the neck of the embarrassed detective.

Lorie and Judy are shouting: "Let's have a big celebration, now!"

Grandpa, full of foresight yet again, is busy designing a beautiful cake in his notebook to bake for the celebration.

Spring has arrived. Orie and Cuddles have become the best of friends. They are quite happy to swap sleeping quarters, so when the hen feels like sleeping in the dog's basket Cuddles readily agrees to go and sleep in the henhouse. But this time, as he settles into the fresh straw, there's something bothering him. He tosses and turns.

"But what is wrong here? Here's an egg! Can it possibly be me...?"

As for Orie, she knew what was going on. At dawn she had laid her first egg, and hurried to her friends right away to tell them all about it.

THE CHILD'S WORLD LIBRARY

THE LOVE AFFAIR OF MR. DING AND MRS. DONG

LULU AND THE ARTIST

THE MAGIC SHOES

THE NEXT BALCONY DOWN

OLD MR. BENNET'S CARROTS

THE RANGER SMOKES TOO MUCH

RIVER AT RISK

SCATTERBRAIN SAM

THE TALE OF THE KITE

TIM TIDIES UP

TOMORROW WILL BE A NICE DAY

THE TREE POACHERS